The New Arrival

Written By Donald Claros

Illustrated by Toby Mikle

THANK YOU!

I would like to thank my wife, my parents, my brothers and sister along with many other individuals who have contributed to my growth as a leader and human being. I would also like to thank all those who serve this great nation and their families. Thank you for everything you do out there to keep us safe.

We love you. To a bright future for you, we will be with you every step of the way. This story is from the heart little one. From your father, mother and big brother, Edgar. Welcome to the world, little Regina.

With the miracle of new life, we wanted to publish this book and serve in a capacity to help a cause. For every sale of a book $1 will be donated to An organization to serve and help others

We always eat dinner as a family,
my father, my mother and I

While mother and father cook dinner, I
set the dinner table and feed our two dogs.
It's just father, mother and I

Mother's enchiladas are the best. Father
and I love them, we have something in
common, my father and I

Sunday is the day my entire family really gets together. My family includes my father, my mother, my cousins, my uncle and my aunt. My family is all together, it is a great day, I love the way things are

During family time, my mother gives my father a little box. It's not his birthday. What is going on? Why a small box?

Father opens the box and inside are little shoes made of cloth. Why is mom giving him little shoes? Everyone is smiling. Why? I do not understand why everyone looks happy

Why is everyone smiling? I am not smiling.
What is happening? Is my family changing?
Is everything changing? Is my world
changing? In my family, there is a total of
3. It is my father, mother and I

I run to my room. I am upset, my world is changing. I am no longer number 1. Now some little person is coming. Coming to take over. I hate what is to come. I have to share my stuff, my legos, my dogs, my room, my father and mother. We are no longer 3

Father knocks on my door, he comes in and sits next to me. Father tells me, "Nothing is changing.". He says, "You are still my number 1". He tells me the new baby is not coming to take my place.

"The new baby is coming to fill your life with joy. You will love being a big brother.

Being the big brother is an amazing thing, you will see. You will teach the baby many new things. I know you will be an amazing brother. You will always be my number 1"

It's 4 months now and mother goes to the doctor. She brings home a picture of the baby inside her belly. I am still mad my world is changing, we are no longer 3

I am not happy, but I am curious. I wonder what the baby looks like. My curiosity is winning. I ask mother to see the picture. I look, and I get a warm feeling inside my heart and my belly. I walk away with a smile, I feel a little happy. I will soon be a big brother, maybe this is not so bad

It is 6 months now, and I am excited to go with mother to the doctor. I want to see how big the baby is. I care about mother and the baby. I make sure mother is eating well. The baby needs to eat so it can grow. I go to all the doctor visits with mother. Soon I will be a big brother

The baby loves watermelon. Dad and I go to the store to get watermelon for mother and the baby. We are still a family of 3

It's 8 months now, my dad and I make room for the baby. We move things out of a room in the house to make room for the baby.

Father and I go shopping to get some paint and some tools to paint the baby's room. This is so exciting, a project just for us to work on

Father, mother and I paint the bedroom, the baby is coming. I am going to be a big brother soon and I am excited, I am happy. Soon we will be 4

Father, mother and I, we drive to the hospital, it's time for the baby. The baby is coming

The baby arrives and father runs to the waiting room to get me. My heart is racing and I am excited. I cannot wait to meet you little one

Father says, "You are now a big brother. After mother, you will be the first person to hold the baby. You will hold the baby even before me, you are still number 1.

I will hold the baby before father, I am still number 1. I hold and hug the baby and the little baby hands hold my fingers. The baby smiles at me. My eyes water and I am very happy. This was a special moment for me. Just the baby and me

I am now officially a big brother. Little one, "I will be the best big brother ever." We were a family of 3 and now we are 4.. My father, my mother, me and the baby. I like these new changes. I am still number 1, but now there is also a number 2

Baby, "I will help take care of you. I promise that I will be a super big brother. I love you little baby."

Made in the USA
Coppell, TX
15 September 2021